Rescued by the Mountain Man – A Short, Steamy Neighbors-to-Lovers Instalove Mountain Man Romance

Mountain Men of Charming Falls, Volume 1

Ann Ric

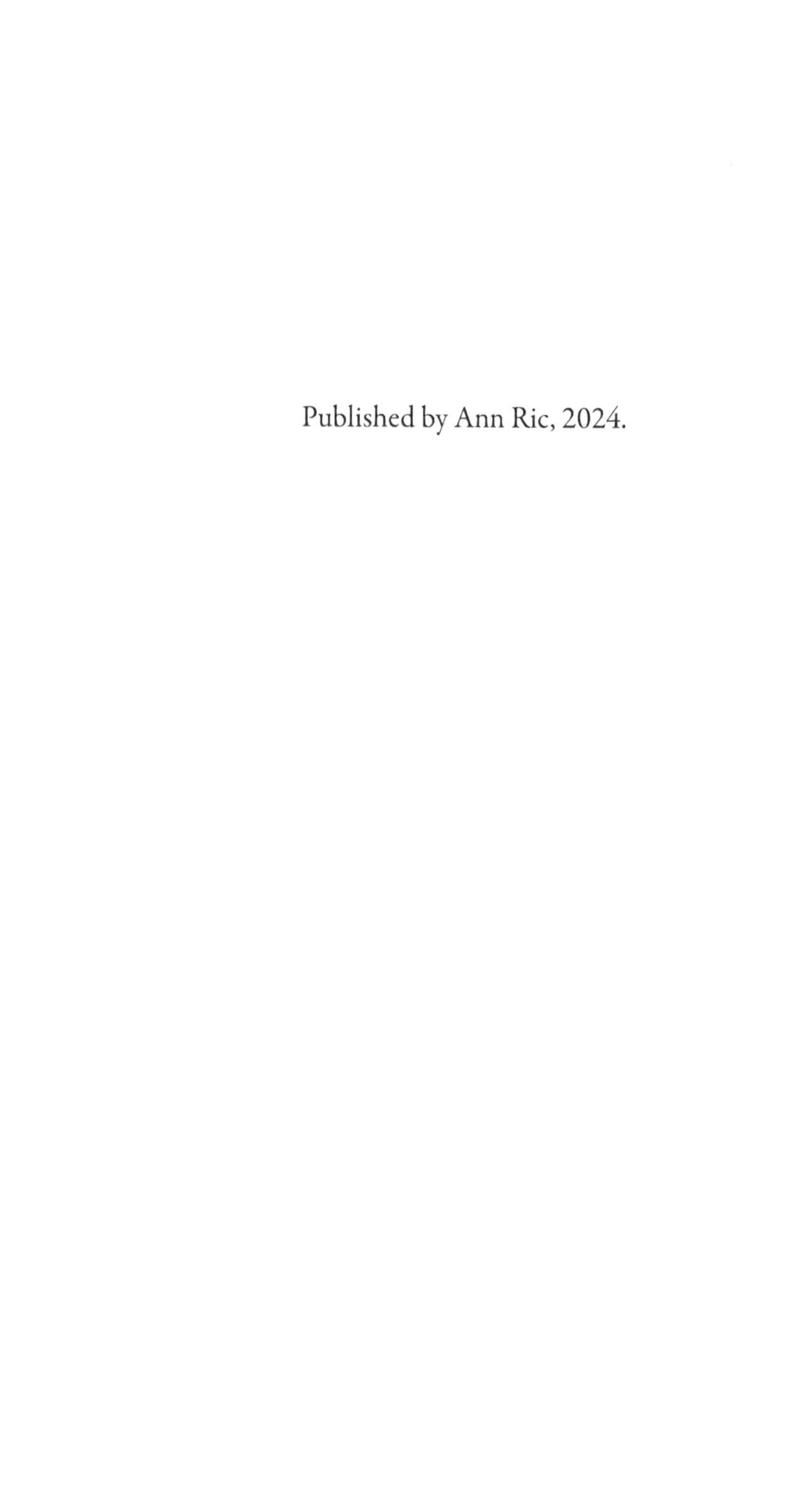

Published by Ann Ric, 2024.

This is a work of fiction. Similarities to real people, places, or events are entirely coincidental.

RESCUED BY THE MOUNTAIN MAN – A SHORT, STEAMY NEIGHBORS-TO-LOVERS INSTALOVE MOUNTAIN MAN ROMANCE

First edition. October 30, 2024.

Copyright © 2024 Ann Ric.

ISBN: 979-8224092260

Written by Ann Ric.

Table of Contents

RESCUED BY THE MOUNTAIN MAN – A Short, Steamy Neighbors-to-Lovers Instalove Mountain Man Romance

Mountain Men of Charming Falls

By Ann Ric

Rescued by the Mountain Man (Mountain Men of Charming Falls)

Rescued by the Mountain Man is a sweet & steamy short instalove romance novella featuring a gorgeous ex-military mountain man and a curvy woman.

Evie is a wedding planner-turned-jilted bride. She became a viral meme when she ran out of the chapel on her wedding day in tears. Why did she live-stream her wedding? Who was she to have it streamed? It wasn't like she was marrying a prince. She'd walked out of her wedding to her now ex-groom when a surprise guest showed up...

His wife!

Yep, that's right. She didn't know her now ex-groom was already married. So much for happily ever after. Humiliated and broken-hearted, she decides to go to a quaint small town where no one knows her; into the woods of the mountain town of Charming Falls to escape. To vanish. To disappear. Until she gets confronted by a bear...

Ex-military soldier and volunteer builder, Jake, wants to escape his past and live alone. Being a recluse in Charming Falls works for him...until a beautiful curvy woman shows up in distress. Will she be the one to break the protective barrier over his heart?

***

Welcome to *Mountain Men of Charming Falls*, the spicy instalove series based on a picturesque small mountain town by a lake that brings you closer to nature. A tranquil scenic escape from the busy city where residents in the cozy close-knit community look out for each other. Let the cool mountain breeze, clear night skies, beautiful romantic sunsets, and the fresh pine scents that fill the air bring you serene relaxation. Known for its camping sites, rustic cabin retreats, hiking trails, ski slopes, and yes, semi-recluse hot and sexy ex-military mountain men who live by the honor code: respect, loyalty, selfless service, integrity and courage in everything they do. Charming Falls is the perfect place to fall in love.

Chapter 1 - Evie

'I need to get away. I need to clear my head," Evie said, tearfully, as she spoke to her friend over the speakerphone in her car while driving on the gravel road.

It was getting late now as she drove through the wooded area near the mountain to find her uncle's empty cabin. The road is somewhere off Cedar Lane. The name of the road is Second Chance Lane. Imagine that. Right now, she didn't think she was ever going to get a second chance at anything. Still, she was grateful for her uncle. He'd told her she could stay there for a while to heal her broken heart and escape the unwanted media frenzy. It was a few weeks before Christmas and this would be the worst Christmas ever.

It had been four weeks now since the now infamous wedding planner walked out on her own wedding before saying her vows as it was live streamed.

She was the laughing stock of social media now. Her business was now defunct in the worst possible way.

"That was so awful what happened to you, girl. I'm so sorry. You didn't deserve that."

"Thanks," Evie said, softly. "Who on earth told me it was a good idea to have my wedding live streamed for the world to watch? It wasn't like I was marrying a prince."

Her friend scuffed. "A prince? Please, the guy's a toad in *this* fairy tale."

On her wedding day, Evie's life, as she knew it, vanished before her eyes and in front of 50,000 followers.

Truth be told she never did feel right about her now ex and now she knew why. She should have followed her instincts and ran when he proposed to her. She should have followed her intuition.

"I've always been known as the overly cautious bore. A no-excitement chick."

"You?"

"Well, that's what my classmates used to call me all throughout high school and college. I always got my homework done early. I never went out to parties. Never smoked or tried any drugs. I was always the do-nothing play-it-safe girl." She sighed. "My dream this year was to do something spontaneous. Something bold. Something exciting that feels right to me. To follow my heart and not miss out. And I thought I could raise money doing it too. And now? It blew up in my face."

"It's not your fault," her friend tried to reassure her.

She had no choice but to walk out on her own live streamed wedding when a surprise guest showed up.

The surprise guest was John's *wife*!

Yep, the toad was already married and forgot to tell Evie. His wife lived in Europe and apparently heard what he was doing and flew over there.

Evie had the idea of live streaming her wedding for her ailing grandmother to see. Her grandmother couldn't leave the hospital so she thought it would be great for her to watch it as she had wanted to see her only grandchild get married.

Evie had also gathered sponsors for her wedding and had made enough to help cover her grandmother's monthly medical expenses. She'd also set up a fund to raise money for those suffering with dementia and mobility ailments. Something her dear grandmother had been diagnosed with and suffered with since her fall two years ago. Her wedding planning business was paying all the bills.

Now?

She was humiliated. Broken hearted. And soon, she'd be broke.

Now no one wanted to trust her with their wedding plans.

She was seen as a bad omen in the wedding industry. Damaged wedding goods.

Rejected so publicly at her own wedding.

That lying two-timer.

Could her life get any worse?

"I'm through with men," Evie declared over the phone as the tires of her car grinded over the gravel road.

"Aww, don't say that, Evie. Not all guys are lying scheming jerks like that creep."

"I know but right now, I'm not willing to give it another chance. Maybe love isn't for everyone."

Her heart sank.

Deep down she'd always wanted to be as happily married as her grandparents were—until her grandfather passed away last year. And she knew her grandmother wanted her to be happily married too.

She sighed deeply, feeling the weight of the world on her shoulders. She also wanted to give deserving brides their beautiful dream wedding and encourage them with their jittering nerves.

She even had a page on her blog titled "How to get over cold feet." She was supposed to be encouraging them that nothing could go wrong on their special day. How was she supposed to do that now? They'd just seen what a disaster her wedding had been. Well, her almost-wedding.

She'd disabled the comments on her blog and social media page, opting to go silent indefinitely.

"Don't say that, girl. You just haven't met the right guy yet. And looks like your luck's about to change."

"Why do you say that?"

"Girl, don't you know about Charming Falls?"

"Yes, of course I do. It's a small mountain town where my uncle has a cabin. I've been here a few times, remember?"

Her heart fluttered in her chest when her mind slid to her uncle's hot and sexy neighbor, Jake. Her uncle once told her that Jake volunteered his time and helped build accessible homes for wounded and disabled vets and their families. And for those who'd lost their homes in storms in nearby towns. He'd do it for almost nothing. Just the cost of the supplies. He could make a killing but he didn't. He was a guy that just did the honorable thing to be of service in his community.

Would she see him again? She hoped she wouldn't see him in the state she was in now. She didn't want to see another guy again. But she couldn't stay in the city. She didn't want to be anywhere near WIFI either.

She was now in Charming Falls, the picturesque small mountain town on a lake that brought you closer to nature. The close-knit community full of locally-owned businesses and plenty of events kept the residents, tourists, nature lovers, hikers and photographers busy. The town's population of 7,000 year-round residents looked out for each other. It was also a tranquil scenic escape from the busy city life. She welcomed the cool mountain breeze and the fresh pine scents that filled the air.

reminding her of simpler times of her childhood when she went on camping trips.

A breath of fresh mountain air was what she needed. She needed to soak in the stunning mountain scenery and enjoy the mountain views.

The town had a cozy familiar feel to it with its beautiful landscapes and the best hiking trails around. Charming Falls High Street was the longest road that ran through the town with a breathtaking view of the mountains and the street was lined with a strip of quaint stores that included locally-owned bakeries with the scent of fresh pastries baked on site, a deli, locally-owned coffee shops with the tastiest freshly brewed coffee, giftshops, bookstores, delicious meals served in the tavern restaurants, chalets, the building supplies store, an art gallery, antique shops, bowling alley, yoga studios, the historic Charming Falls Inn, and of course the Charming Falls Cozy Bar & Grill that attracted many tourists.

Everybody loved visiting Charming Falls. And yes, the female visitors loved glancing at the hot mountain men who lived on the mountains in their rustic log cabins.

Many were ex-military men; war vets who worked in the town or volunteered their time helping out in the district while living off the land. Many still lived by their honor and protect code from their time in the military. And they were sexy as hell, so deliciously handsome they had the female tourists ogling their muscular fit bodies; the men spent most of their time doing physical work on the mountains and in their community.

Everyone knew each other in the town *and* each other's business. But she couldn't think about that right now. She just hoped they all didn't have WIFI and knew what went down on the Internet. Still, the residents all looked out for one another.

There were plenty of secluded log cabins on the mountains.

It was a perfect quiet escape with the most breathtaking views of nature. She needed that to clear the air. To clear her thoughts. To process her next move.

A person could easily get lost in the woods on the mountains if they weren't careful. There were so many small winding roads. Charming Falls had small-town charm with its pristine lakes and amazing mountains but man, did they have a lot of small winding dirt roads. The roads all looked the same.

Her friend chuckled. "Girl, you are in for a treat. Heard there's a lot of hot mountain men up there. And I mean so hot, the ice on the mountain could melt under their hotness. And they're all like honorable and shit like that. Most of them are ex-military soldiers. And *fit*."

Evie grinned and shook her head. "You've got to be kidding me. That's all you can think about is how hot and fit they are.?"

"Of course," her friend said, shamelessly. "Sometimes hot recluse ex-soldiers make the best lovers. It's raining mountain men, girl. You'd better leave your umbrella at home. That's the best way to get over your ex."

"Very funny. But I'm not into one-night stands." Evie playfully rolled her eyes. "Thanks for trying to cheer me up but I'm *really* through with men for now. Charming or not."

"You don't really mean that."

"Of course I do," Evie teased, shaking her head. "Thanks for being a good friend. But like I said, I'm on a break from men—even mountain men from Charming Falls."

"Just call me when you get there, hon," her friend said.

"Thanks, you're a solid friend," Evie said again. What would she do if she didn't have her friend to talk to right now. She felt so alone. So humiliated. So broken.

"Hey, no worries. And no more tears for that jerk, okay? He's not worth it. You're always there for everyone else. You need a break, girl. Who cares what anyone else thinks."

Unfortunately, I do.

No matter how much she told herself it didn't matter what others thought of her or her "sham business" as they now called it online, it *did* hurt. Words hurt her like a rock. She'd tried so hard to make it in the wedding planning business. She wanted to help deserving brides and grooms have a special day to remember. The irony was not lost on her that *she* was the one who would have a wedding day to remember—on the internet for the rest of her life!

Imagine a wedding planner having the most disastrous wedding in the history of weddings in that town. How could her business ever recover?

Image was everything and the image over the internet of her wedding day was anything but cool.

And her grandmother was so heartbroken over it too, which made it even worse.

Her business was over. She was now unemployed. The cancellations of her wedding planning services came in like a flood.

But nothing hurt more than John's betrayal.

What an idiot she had been to believe him.

What an idiot *he* was.

She'd made a list a long time ago about what she wanted in a man. He had to be:

1. *Sweet and sexy*
2. *Loves me for who I am*
3. *Passionate kisser*
4. *Great in bed*
5. *Makes my heart race, he takes my breath away*
6. *Strong and kind*
7. *Great in the kitchen, not just the bedroom*
8. *A great listener*
9. *Faithful and honest to the core*

She laughed at the thought now. Her ex was none of that. The last item on the list was so important too. Being faithful and honest. Her ex was a con artist. Plain and simple. A would-be bigamist. What did she ever see in him? Maybe she was expecting too much. If a guy couldn't be faithful to her, well, there was no way she'd stay with him.

After she ended her phone call with her friend, Evie narrowed her eyes, looking for her uncle's old cabin as she drove slowly on the dirt road.

Second Chance Lane must be around there somewhere.

Unfortunately, the exact location wasn't on the map, so she had to figure it out based on his instructions. Her uncle had left the state a while ago and was spending more time down south in the warmer weather. Her uncle had no children of his own and always treated her like a daughter.

Just then, she saw a creature run in front of her car and swerve so she wouldn't hit the little thing. Was it a squirrel or a beaver? She couldn't tell and didn't know if these small animals even lived around that neck of the woods.

Unfortunately, her car swerved and took a nose dive into a ditch with a thump sound as it hit a tree.

"Oh, great. I'm in the ditch. Much like my career now," she whispered to herself, breathing hard, her heartbeat pounding in her chest.

She heard a horrible sound erupt from the engine. Her car wasn't exactly new but she loved old Tom. Yep, she named her car Tom. At least, *he* was reliable and never lied to her. He was there when she needed. And she took great care of him.

Unfortunately, this accident looked like it would be the straw that broke its back.

Evie surveyed her car when she got out. The front was totalled.

She reached into her phone and read the screen in horror.

No service.

Oh, great.

Her heart leaped with anxiety in her chest.

She was in an area of the mountains that had weak cell phone signal.

What a great spot to have your car break down, she thought with an air of sarcasm.

She was hoping to charge it once she reached the cabin but right now she didn't know *when* she'd reach it and she couldn't call her friend back to tell her she was stuck in the mountains. No one would find her or know what happened to her.

The sun was beginning to set.

Evie didn't have much time before dark. She had no idea just how far the cabin was from there but she had no choice but to walk to the nearest civilization. She knew it would be way too dangerous to stay there and hope someone spotted her.

The first rule of camping was to make sure you could get help—if needed. She'd heard that a signal mirror could be seen up to a hundred miles away. She would need some sort of survival reflective signal mirror to reflect the sunlight and alert any potential rescuers, or some sort of beacon to alert help.

But then again, what if she ended up alerting wild animals like bears or wolves instead of help?

Her heart thumped hard in her chest at the thought.

She was so screwed.

Okay, Evie, you'll be okay. Just keep walking. Your uncle's cabin can't be that far from here.

That's what she hoped. But as she took each step, her hope faded. All the small dirt roads looked the same around there. And without access to her GPS, she had no idea how close she was. The roads weren't even on the Google map.

"Ouch." She stepped on a broken tree branch and scraped her ankle. Now she was hobbling as she walked.

Man, she must look like quite a sight.

A chill came around her then...

She heard a sound.

It was the type of sound that made the hairs on your skin stand up.

She heard a low growl from an animal and felt a presence as the cracking sound of someone or something stepping on tree branches on the ground could be heard. When she turned around, a large grizzly bear stood a few feet away from her.

Her breath caught in her throat. Panic swept over her spine.

Her instinct was to run but she'd heard it was best to stay calm.

Well, how on earth could she stay calm at a time like this?

Her eyes widened in terror.

Her pulse fired up.

She must have been shaking in her boots because the bear kept staring at her while inching closer.

Oh, no.

Her life was so over now.

Chapter 2 - Jake

Jake had just finished chopping wood and was about to head back to his cabin on the mountain.

He wiped a sweat from his brow and got back into his pick-up truck. He and his army buddies lived on the mountains and were okay with the isolation. They'd made a pack a long time ago that they'd go it alone.

Like his friends, they'd had their share of heartbreak and not fitting in to city life, especially after their last tour of duty. They spent most of their time volunteering in the small mountain town of Charming Falls where they'd settled, helping to build accessible homes or repair rooftops damaged in the storms. He kept this distance from most people though.

People couldn't be trusted, at least not in the corporate world where he'd tried to fit in. He was a hands-on guy and liked to work with his hands. He never did fit in with the office.

He'd served his time overseas defending his country and did his part. He was glad to do it but his emotional injuries would probably never heal. Coming back and making his way in the corporate world was another war zone. One he didn't like.

And while he was serving overseas, his now ex-fiancée was cheating on him with her boss—his old school friend. So much for trust. He'd asked his friend to look after his fiancée while he was away—not to screw her.

He was so angry he could have kicked that guy's ass but he didn't.

Still, he didn't have much time to dwell on the past. He was okay being away from everyone and he loved being out in the woods, just him and nature. The cabins were spread out far from each other so it wasn't as if he saw anyone. He'd go in to town for a beer at the Charming Falls Cozy Bar and Grill with the guys once a week but that was it.

His life was in the woods now—up in the mountains.

As he drove along the dirt road he thought he heard a scream in the distance.

He slowed his truck down to a stop then switched off the engine.

The sound of a woman in distress echoed.

He started up his engine and immediately turned his truck around to the direction of the sound.

Before long, he found the source of the scream.

He saw a curvy woman clutching her handbag to her chest, confronted by a bear.

He made a loud noise by slamming the door of his truck and shouted, "Hey! Go away!"

The bear was startled by his voice, quickly turned around and went the other direction.

The woman looked relieved and breathed a sigh of relief.

She turned around to face him.

His heart stopped in his chest.

It was the first time he got a good look of her beautifully-angelic face.

She was breathtaking.

Stunning. And man, she had curves in all the right places. He loved a woman that filled out nicely in her outfit. Butterflies slid inside his belly.

Just then recognition hit him.

He knew her.

She was his neighbor Ted's niece.

Damn. He'd seen her from afar before but never got a good look at her until now.

His groin reacted just now to his surprise. He hoped he could control his body's response to this vision of loveliness. She had beautiful ebony silky hair, large brown eyes and a sweet oval face with pouty red lips. She looked like a curvy goddess. He was mesmerized by her breath-taking beauty.

"Wow! Thank you so much," she said, breathing hard. "Does shouting 'go away' always work?"

"Not for humans," he said. Not sure why he said that but it caused her lips to curve into a lovely smile.

She then tilted her head back and laughed. "I hear you," she said.

He loved the sound of her sweet angelic voice. It resonated within him like a sweet harmony.

Considering what she'd just been through earlier, he was pleasantly surprised at how she took it all in stride.

"I'm Evie," she said and held out her hand. "Thank you again for saving my life."

She then stopped. "Wait a minute. Aren't you..."

"I'm Jake," he said. "I'm your uncle's neighbor on Second Chance Lane. I live in the cabin to his right. And hey, it's no worries. Glad I was here."

He took her hand in his and butterflies exploded in his belly. She was stunning, her skin so smooth to touch. The scent of her sweet perfume wafted to his nostrils. He'd never been this close to her before. They'd only waved in passing once when she'd visited her uncle in the past.

Just then their eyes locked and he felt a sweet sensation slide down his spine as he held her hand for a brief moment.

Her hand felt soft yet strong.

Okay, it was time to let go. They'd shook hands for a lot longer than required as if they'd become glued to each other all of a sudden.

For a moment, there was an awkward pause between them.

Chapter 3 - Evie

"You need some help?" Jake, the strikingly good-looking and physically fit mountain man, asked her. His beautiful eyes darted over to her car in the ditch. Heat climbed to her cheeks as he neared her, leaving her feeling breathless.

Man, his voice was so deep, commanding and sensuous. He also wore a serious expression on his gorgeous face. She couldn't quite read him.

He had the most stunning features she'd ever seen on a man. A sexy stubble, high chiseled cheekbones and strong handsome facial features. She could look at him all day. She was surprised at her body's instant response to him. This had never happened before, not even with her ex.

She'd never gotten this close to Jake before. Her uncle's cabin wasn't exactly next door. The cabins were so far spread out and surrounded by pine trees that she'd have to walk a few minutes to get to the next cabin. But man, he was hot and sexy. Broad shoulders and slim waist. He was a lot taller than she'd thought now she was up close to him.

His voice stirred a reaction in her. It slid through her like sweet warm honey. And she caught a sweet cologne scent from him.

Okay, stop ogling him, Evie. He's just a guy that saved your life and asked if you need help. He's probably taken. All the good ones are. And besides, you're on a break from men, remember?

"Yes, as a matter of fact, I do," she finally said, sheepishly.

"What happened here?" He surveyed the damage to her vehicle.

"I thought I saw a squirrel run across the road and tried to avoid him."

"Oh, no."

"Oh, yes. And unfortunately, I couldn't avoid the *tree*."

"I'll have the guys tow it to the garage in town."

"You will? Thank you so much."

"Do you live around here?"

"No, I was on my way to my uncle's cabin. I'm supposed to be spending some time there while he's away."

"Yeah, he's a cool dude. Your uncle talks highly of you, whenever we meet up in the town. Just let me know if you need anything while you're out here."

Warmth crept over her.

"My uncle speaks highly of you too. He told me you help him out a lot. I guess we have Uncle Ted in common," she said, fumbling for words.

Why on earth was she so tongue-tied all of a sudden?

She couldn't remember when she last felt this way around a guy. But then again, Jake wasn't just any guy.

Relief washed over her. And she suddenly felt relaxed around him.

Even though she'd just met Jake up close for the first time, she knew a lot about him. Her uncle had told her so much about the nice neighbor that always gave him a helping hand. He also mentioned his neighbor was a recluse that didn't have many visitors at all, except for an older relative that visited once in a while.

At least Jake's character had been vetted by her uncle. And her uncle, who used to work in law enforcement, was a man that didn't trust easily. He always observed people and their character.

"I'll take you to his cabin, if you like."

"Please, that would be great. Hopefully, my uncle has good reception so I can use my cell phone."

"Yeah, you have to be careful out here. The phones don't always work depending on what area you're in."

"How do you manage to live out here?" she asked.

He shrugged. "You get used to it. I don't mind being closer to nature."

Just like her uncle. She understood why some people wanted to live away from the city and the drama and just be surrounded by nature and tranquility. But she didn't think she could ever be one of them. She liked being close to various amenities. It was her life.

Jake noticed her limping and the look of concern spread across his handsome face.

"You okay?" he asked with concern, glancing at her ankle.

"I'm fine. I just scraped my ankle against a fallen branch."

"I'll take a look at that," he said, offering his strong arm. She held unto him as he helped her up to his SUV. Once she was in the passenger side, he closed the door for her. He then went to his trunk to pull out a First Aid kit.

She liked his chivalry. And his scent. It was so irresistible. But she had to get hold of herself. Her uncle would not approve of her getting too close to his neighbor. He always liked to keep to himself. He said it's good to live well with your neighbors but you didn't have to be in their pockets.

He then returned to her side with the First Aid kit.

"Man, you're really prepared," she observed.

"Got to be prepared for anything up here," he replied as he tended to her.

She grinned, appreciatively. His firm soft hands touched her ankle as he cleaned her scratch with saline then bandaged it up. Her pussy throbbed at his touch and yet he was only touching her ankle. There was something sweet and sexy about his touch. What was with her? She'd only seen Jake a few times. But oh, she wanted to see more of him.

"Thank you for doing that," she said, her voice a little hoarser than she'd intended. She hoped he didn't smell her arousal because oh, her panties were moist right now.

"No problem."

And she was really grateful for his care just now. His skin was so gentle. She eyed the impressive muscles on his biceps with admiration. He was well built in all the right places.

Ten minutes later, they'd driven on the gravel road towards her uncle's cabin. She didn't realize how close she had been before.

When they arrived, her jaw fell wide open.

***

"Oh, my god! What happened?" she said, after Jake helped her out of his SUV.

Jake furrowed his brows and walked up to the cabin as water seeped through the front door.

"It could be from a burst pipe," he said. He went back to his SUV and pulled out his boots and put them on.

He then searched around for her uncle's spare key under a rock and then let himself in. "Your uncle told me where to find his spare key so I can check on his cabin when there's a storm or outage when he's not here."

"It's a good thing." Evie was still in shock and almost forgot that she'd had a spare key to her uncle's cabin too.

Jake moved closer to the front door. "Stay here," he said to her, making sure there was no danger.

He then opened the door and more water spilled out.

"Oh, no. There's going to be so much water damage," she said, alarmed.

"My men and I will take care of it," Jake said, calmly. His voice was so reassuring, so controlled. "No need to worry," he added.

"I have nowhere to stay," she said as she fought to stop her lips from trembling but it was no use. Her day could not have gotten any worse. Now where would she stay? She couldn't drive back to the city tonight.

"You can stay in my cabin. I've got a spare room," he said, reassuringly.

"Oh, no. I...I can't put you out."

That was the last thing she would want to do. She didn't know her uncle's neighbor that well.

"Hey, it's no trouble at all. You can't stay here. The place is flooded."

He then pulled out his cell phone.

"I don't have a signal yet but I'm going to send a text to my guys to meet me up here. We'll have it sorted out soon. They'll get the message when the servers back up."

Appreciation filled her.

"Thanks so much, Jake." He came back out of her uncle's cabin.

"You're so well-equipped," she said and then almost bit her own tongue for saying that. She didn't mean his body—although he was well-equipped. She was referring to his SUV. Looked like he had everything stocked in there.

"I'm always prepared out here. You never know when the weather will turn or if emergencies prop up."

"Of course," she said, softly. And she wanted to add that his military training probably had a lot to do with his preparedness too, but she didn't say that. She always admired the way soldiers were always prepared—for anything. Getting caught off guard was not a good thing. She wished she had been prepared for this. Thank god Jake had come to her rescue. Yet again.

Chapter 4 - Jake

"I'm really sorry about your uncle's place," Jake said as they walked into his own log cabin not far from Ted's place.

The sad expression on Evie's pretty face felt like a gut punch. He didn't know why but it troubled him to see this angelic woman so upset. She was way too pretty to be unhappy. He wished he could make it all better for her.

A sudden urge to protect her swept over him.

A sudden urge to be *inside* her came over him. He was so drawn to her like a moth to a flame. And she was hot.

Stop those thoughts, Jake. She's your neighbor's niece. Jake tried to control where his mind was going, captivated by this stunning beauty before him.

"We had a lot of heavy rain fall recently," he added, shifting his focus back to the moment.

"It looks as if the storm cloud hung over my uncle's cabin the whole time," she said, her lips pouted. Those lips. Wow, her lips were so shapely, so sexy. But he had to tear his gaze away from her. She was off-limits. She was his neighbor's niece. His neighbor, the ex-law enforcement officer would not like this one bit. He knew Ted. Plus, the mountains were his life now. The last thing he would want would be to have any awkwardness with his neighbors around there.

He grinned at her words. Man, she had a sense of humor.

"Sorry about that," he said.

"It's okay, it's not your fault. Unless you had something to do with the rain cloud."

He arched a brow and grinned. It took a lot to make him grin. She was cute and funny.

"That's one thing I can't control," he joked. He also couldn't control his feelings around Ms Evie. He'd only just met her, yet there was something about her that resonated with him. He never believed in all this talk of instant attraction and chemistry before—until now. But he had to focus and change the subject fast.

"Did your uncle have insurance?"

"I think so. I'm not sure if it lapsed though. I know he told me he was having trouble with the insurance company. God, I hope he's still covered."

"Don't worry. Even if he isn't. My guys will sort something out and see how we can help."

"I really appreciate that, Jake."

"Let me fix you something to eat. You must be hungry," he said.

"That's very kind of you." She looked around. He noticed her eyes light up when she took in the surroundings of his cozy cabin.

"Your place is so impressive," she said, glancing around with approval. "I love the rustic look, the polished hardwood floors and the cozy decor. It's a little different from my uncle's cabin."

"Thanks," he said. "It's okay."

"Oh, it's more than okay. I love it."

"I'm glad you do."

He paused for a moment. "I'll show you around soon. But for now, you must be hungry. What can I make you?"

"Whatever you're having," she said. "I really appreciate it, Jake." Her voice sounded sweet and humble. Her sweetness gave him a warm feeling inside him like he'd do anything for her.

"Like I said, it's no trouble at all."

Jake soon busied himself in the kitchen getting pots and pans from the cupboard. He then started to make dinner. He already had seasoned boneless skinless chicken pieces marinating in the fridge. He took them out and added them to the baking pan and placed them in the oven. It should be done in about thirty minutes.

"The view is gorgeous," she said, looking out the window.

Jake had to agree with her as he stood behind her, his eyes surveyed her rounded ass while she faced the window. His cock moved.

Okay, what was happening here? Why was he so drawn to this lovely woman?

Because she was delightful. She was different. She radiated something he'd never seen before from a woman. She was innocent. Caring. Kind.

He swallowed hard. "Yes, it is," he finally said.

"It's so calm and relaxing out here," she said, moving closer to the window. "Just nature. I love it. So much quieter and relaxing than the city."

"No better place than the mountains," he agreed.

"You can say that again."

"So what made you decide to come to the mountains?" he asked her once they'd settled in the living room.

She looked down for a moment. Her cheeks flushed.

Oh, no. Did he ask the wrong question? He didn't spend a lot of time around people—especially women. His social conversation skills could probably use a little work.

"I guess you don't have internet around here, so you didn't see it," she finally said.

"See what?" he asked.

"The worst wedding ceremony on the planet."

"Oh, no. What happened? Your wedding was ruined?" His heart lunged in his chest. He knew he was supposed to *look out* for his neighbor's niece, not *check her out*, but he didn't know she was married.

His gut clenched.

Why did disappointment flood through him? It wasn't as if he would be dating her.

"No, my wedding wasn't ruined, my wedding never *happened.*"

"What happened?" he inquired, carefully. "Other than your wedding not happening," he added.

Now it was her turn to grin but soon that grin was replaced by a frown. "His wife showed up," she blurted out, matter-of-factly.

"What?" Jake was stunned into silence for a moment. "Your groom was already *married*?" Fury shot through Jake's vein. He felt angry for poor little Evie. What kind of low-life creep would do that to her?

She nodded slowly, biting down on her plump lower lip.

She looked so adorable when she did that. But then his cock jumped. He had to get a hold of himself. She looked too sexy when she pouted her shapely lips.

Jake heard about a poor bride who ran out of the church in tears after her groom's wife appeared. He had no idea it was his neighbor's niece.

Man, he wished he could have been there to give that asshole groom of hers a piece of his mind. That was no way to treat a lady. No woman deserved that. His wife *or* his bride-to-be, since neither knew the other existed.

He had a word for assholes like that who'd pull a stunt like that on a woman and it wasn't pretty. Evie didn't deserve that. No woman did. He just wanted to reach out to her. To protect her. To make it all right for her. Heck, he'd spent most of his time being a recluse but he did check out what's happening online from time to time. He had to make sure his business interests were doing okay.

He made her some coffee while they waited for the chicken to cook in the oven and was glad the fridge was stocked. It was as if the universe knew he'd have company today.

He listened as she spoke about what happened.

Before long they were talking for an hour. He really enjoyed her company and her energies. People carried a vibe about them without realizing it. And her vibes connected with him. Though he was deeply sorry for all the shit she'd just been through.

"I guess I'm a screw up," Evie said, "Always making mistakes." She sighed deeply as she held onto her mug of coffee.

"You're not a screw up," he said, firmly. "I think it was George Bernard Shaw that said something like 'a life spent making mistakes is not only more honorable, but more useful than a life spent doing nothing.'"

Her eyes misted over.

"You okay?" he asked her.

"Sorry, but that was beautiful. That was the sweetest thing I've heard in a long while. Thank you for your kind words."

"It's not my words but it's my sentiment. And it's true. Don't let anyone tell you otherwise. I admire the way you handled yourself."

"By running away?"

"No, by taking charge and taking a break to recharge."

Their gaze locked for a moment. His cock hardened in his pants again. He hoped she didn't see that. He positioned himself behind the counter in the kitchen so she couldn't see his midsection. Why was he so turned on by her? He really liked her. A lot. And he hadn't even known her that long. It took a lot for Jake to warm up to anyone. And right now, he was hot for Evie. But she'd just came out of a relationship. And he had vowed to never get back into one.

Chapter 5 - Evie

"You are an amazing cook, Jake," Evie said, later that evening. "The dinner was delicious!"

She could not believe how skilled Jake was in the kitchen. She'd heard about ex-soldiers and their abilities to be good at pretty much everything. When they were out on the frontlines or living in foreign territories they had to know how to survive. But she had no idea just how talented he was in the kitchen.

And probably in the bedroom too.

What was wrong with her? She could not believe that naughty thought slid into her mind. But there was just something different about Jake. She had to get her mind out of that area fast. Jake was a gorgeous strong man but he was off limits. So off limits. And it had only been a month since her break up from her ex.

"Glad you like it," he said, finishing up. She watched as he tidied up, his strong muscles flexing.

She offered to help tidy up but he said he would have none of that. He'd told her she was his guest.

His log cabin was immaculate. It was so spacious and clean. She'd never met a man who kept such a tidy place before. Not that she had much experience. Her ex-fiancé was her first real boyfriend and they hadn't known each other long. In fact, they hadn't known much about each other at all, it seemed.

Still, she loved the rustic charm, the polished hardwood floors, the cozy stone fireplace in the living room and the comfy rug in the center. The tall windows let in a scenic view of the outside as the sun began to set. It was so welcoming. So relaxing.

But the energies were nothing compared to the energies coming from Jake. He had something about him that made her drawn to him. Probably because he was an honorable man. He oozed it. So opposite of her slimy lying ex. Jake was the real deal. She could just feel that coming from him.

"Well, thank you again," she said.

"It was no trouble at all. It's only dinner." He turned to face her and their eyes locked into a gaze. She felt heat climb to her cheeks. Why was she getting hot inside all of a sudden. The space between her legs throbbed. She was so drawn to him.

Funny thing was that she was never drawn to her ex. Her ex never made her heart leap in her chest or butterflies spring into her belly. Not like the way she was feeling with Jake. This man had a sweet chemical effect on her.

"Well, it was a lot more than dinner. Thank you for everything. For listening to me drone on about my problems. I mean, you really have good listening skills." He nodded at the right moments and voiced his thoughts, showed a lot of empathy. Something she never got from her ex. He could easily be a therapist. She felt so seen, so understood, so relieved after getting so much off her chest.

"No one's ever told me that before." He arched his brow and held her gaze for a moment before motioning to the living room.

They both made their way to the living area.

"Well, you do and I appreciate it. It means a lot to be able to get that off my chest." She seriously had never dated a guy like that before who would take the time to listen actively and with such empathy. He really made her feel important. And yet she'd only just spent a day with him. Sure, she'd seen him from afar before and she knew of him but this was the first time she'd actually spent time with him.

"So what about you?" she asked him. "Do you live out here alone?" she asked him.

Okay, she could totally kick herself. Why did she ask him that? Her uncle had told her that he lived alone. Still, she was curious to find out if he was seeing someone.

He bristled. "Yep. It's just me here."

She sensed he had something on his chest.

"I bought a house in the city with my ex-fiancée."

"Oh," she said, listening with attentiveness.

"But she had other plans."

"What do you mean?"

"While I was serving my last tour, she was...well, she'd found someone else."

Her heart squeezed in her chest. "Oh, no. That's awful. I'm so sorry you went through that," she said, knowing how it felt to have your heart smashed by the one you thought was your soul mate.

"Well, she moved on and so did I." He paused for a moment. "And yes, I gave her the house. She has a kid from a previous relationship. I didn't want to see her kid get shuffled around as she tried to find new housing."

"That was very..."

"Stupid?" he said, arching a brow.

"No! I was going to say, *kind* of you." Heat climbed to her chest. To think that her ex had always insisted on splitting every restaurant bill, even though he ate more than she did. And here was Jake giving up his home to his ex instead of splitting it down the middle and taking his share. "That was very noble of you.

Your ex didn't deserve you." Jake had every right to go after his half of their property but he took the high road and walked away from all of that. Her uncle was right about him. Noble to a fault. But there was such sweetness beyond his tough exterior.

"It wasn't worth the trouble. Besides, I was needed out here. At that time, one of my fellow soldiers who lost a limb while serving was having trouble. My buddies and I rallied around him to help him rebuild his home here in Charming Falls. That's when I knew this was the place for me. Everyone was true out here. No backstabbing or lies. Just plain country folks who tell it like it is."

She smiled warmly. "Yes, the mood out here is different in Charming Falls. My uncle told me this place was like a breath of fresh mountain air. The people are as charming as the name of the town and they look out for each other out here."

"You've got that right."

"So do you work out here too?"

"I spend most of my time volunteering. I'll take you into town if you like. How long are you here for?"

She paused for a moment. She would love to be here for longer than she'd planned. But her uncle's cabin was a lot smaller than Jake's cabin. Her uncle only had one room. Where would she stay? The warm glow from the fireplace made Jake's features even more handsome. It was refreshing being around a good man. And oh, she was aroused by his sexiness.

Right now, he wore a T-shirt and blue jeans. He filled out nicely in his clothes. She admired the decorated tattoos that ran down his muscular sculpted arms. She could see the definition of his muscular chest and wondered what he would be like in bed. Why was her mind going there? It wasn't like they would ever be intimate. Oh, who was she kidding? God, she would love to feel his body over hers tonight. If only.

Desire for him coursed through her body. Was this what love at first sight felt like?

How long could she stay locked up with sexy Jake when her love hormones were out of control around this guy?

Chapter 6 - Jake

Later that night, after a tour of Jake's cabin, Evie settled into the guest room. Their fingers brushed when he'd handed her some fluffy cream-colored towels for her shower later.

Electricity pulsed between them and he saw her cheeks turn red.

There was chemistry there. But he had to shift his focus. She needed his help—not his cock. That wasn't why she found her way in his neck of the woods.

If her uncle's cabin hadn't been flooded, she'd be there now—not at his cabin. Temptation was a killer right now. Man, his body wanted her. *He* wanted her. She was so precious and good-natured. He loved everything about her aura. Her body. Oh, that sexy curvaceous body of hers. And she carried herself as if she didn't realize how hot she was. Beautiful inside and outside. Humble and sweet. He'd never met a woman like that before.

Earlier she'd told him all about her troubles with her wedding and how the social media sponsors were helping her pay for her grandmother's monthly medical care. What a sweetheart Evie was. He was sorry that she'd lost some of her sponsors since the fiasco but it wasn't her fault. Why should she have to pay for that. He figured some rest and relaxation there in Charming Falls would do her some good. That small mountain town was a great place for anyone to clear their mind. It did him a world of good.

"Is everything all right?" she asked him.

"Yes, I just got a call from Alex, one of my army buddies. He's at the cabin now. Chase and Dale will be over there too so we can help get things taken care of.

"That is so sweet of you all. I don't know how to thank you."

"Hey, it's no trouble. It's what we do."

"I'd love to meet your friends to thank them too. My uncle would be so appreciative."

A grin curved his lips. Her appreciation was sweet. His ex had always taken him for granted. He'd rarely heard a word of thanks coming from his ex's lips. He'd wondered now how they'd lasted as long as they did.

But Evie was so thankful. This little pretty angel's heart was filled with gratitude even for the simplest things. He loved that about her.

He also had to stop looking at her lips and her curves or he'd get aroused again.

"So who else lives around here?" she asked him.

"A few of the guys I served with overseas."

"Oh," she said, showing interest.

"Yeah."

"I think it's wonderful what you've all done for your country," she added.

"It's a great honor to serve," he said.

Jake didn't want to add that the pain and agony he and his men had been through or the horrors they'd seen had been unbearable. The uncertainty of not knowing if they'd be coming back home to their country. They served with honor and they were proud of their service. But it was time to move forward now. Many of his men were not as fortunate and had sustained lifelong injuries.

He was all too willing to do what he could to help out. And he and some of his men set up an organisation to help disabled vets and their families.

***

Two hours later, Jake had made sure Evie was secure and safe and left her at his cabin while he and the others went over to Ted's cabin.

"Well, you look like you've seen an angel," Erik said, narrowing his eyes with suspicion. "You just got laid?"

"Nope," Jake said, hoping he wouldn't flush thinking about seeing Evie again. The truth was he would love to lay sweet Evie down on his king-sized bed, spread her legs apart and make love to her over and over again.

"You met someone then," Chase added.

"What is this? The third degree?" Jake said, grinning.

"You're not so uptight tonight," Erik teased him.

"Am I ever uptight?" Jake said.

"You've got a spring in your step, man," Erik added. "Who's the lucky girl?"

The guys all knew what Jake had been through with his ex and he'd sworn he'd be a bachelor for the rest of his life. But he'd never met anyone like Evie until tonight.

"Ted's niece is over at my cabin," Jake finally said.

"Hey, nice," Chase nudged him.

"It's not like that. You know Ted will kill me if I even think about dating his niece. Anyway, she had no other place to stay as you can see. How long do you think it'll take." Jake surveyed the damage to the cabin.

"A good while. Did you get a hold of Ted yet?"

"Nope. His cell's out. The storm in Florida's not helping."

"Ah, right."

"Well, let's get on with the show."

The guys spent the next few hours doing what they could to start the cleanup in Ted's cabin. It was going to be a while before anyone could move back in there.

He didn't know when this would be ready to be inhabited again.

Would this mean he'd see more of Evie? But how was he going to keep from getting too close to her?

Chapter 7 - Jake

Jake kept thinking about Evie. He obsessed over her while he spent time working on her uncle's cabin.

Later, he and the guys went down to the Charming Falls Cozy Bar and Grill to have a drink. But the lovely curvy princess was all he could think about.

Music played in the background as he sat at the bar with his friends. The sound of laughter and chatter came from the patrons at the other tables. It was a rustic cozy environment that brought tourists from all over the country. The light was dim and the mood was always mellow at the Cozy Bar and Grill, the perfect place to chill after a long day or evening at work.

It was as if his friends knew he was thinking about his neighbor's niece because they made comments about him looking like a man in love. Had Evie really made that impact on him?

His friends told him he had changed. His moods had changed. He had more spirit in his steps. He was more energized.

He noticed it too.

"Hey man, don't fight it," Erik said to him.

"Don't fight what?" Jake took a swig of his drink.

"You're attraction to this earth angel. You said you'd never be in a relationship again but tonight you seem like a whole new person. Whoever this woman is, man she has you." Erik grinned.

"I'm not sure about that. I've only seen her a few times. I know a lot about her from her uncle Ted but..."

"But what?" Erik said, arching a brow. "You think she's anything like your ex?"

Jake's friend Erik was protective of his army buddies and he'd been through his own share of heartbreak in the past. Yet, he wanted to see his mates settle down, even if he didn't think he ever would.

"Hey, Evie is nothing like my ex," Jake said. "Not even a little bit. She's a kind-hearted sweet beautiful woman who I happen to like as a neighbor. I don't want anything to ruin that."

But then the thought of Evie being with someone else drove him crazy. What if Erik was right? What if he didn't pursue it and someone else snatched her up. And worse, someone like her creepy ex who defiled her reputation.

He'd go insane if anything like that ever happened to sweet Evie again. He felt as if he'd known her forever since her uncle doted over her and always spoke highly of her over the years. She was the type of girl that always checked on her uncle and called him to see how he was doing—every chance she got. Ted had told him that Evie remembered every holiday and special occasion and spoke to him to make sure he was never alone—even though she was busy looking after her grandmother on her other side of the family—not to mention running an online business. Yes, Evie deserved the best in life. She had a heart of gold. And Jake wanted a place in her heart. But how could this work?

Chapter 8 - Evie

It was two in the morning when Jake had gotten back to his cabin. The light was on in the living room. He thought Evie had gone to bed.

"Hey you, what are you doing up?" he said.

"I couldn't sleep. But something you said made me realize I should plan for a comeback in my business." She sat by the fireplace with her laptop open, glad she was able to get some WIFI for the moment. She then closed it down and snapped her MacBook shut.

"Good on you," he said, inching closer to her. "I knew you could do it. You have more power in you than you realize, Evie. You're a smart beautiful girl."

His words caused ripples of pleasure to run down her spine. She could tell he meant what he said when he captured her gaze with his.

"Thank you," she said, swallowing hard. Her breath shallow now. She could feel her nipples strain underneath her nightie. "Thank you for everything. And...how is my uncle's cabin?" She bit down on her lower lip.

She noticed his gaze drop to her lips and butterflies exploded in her belly at his stunning look.

"Everything's good. It's going to be a while though before you can stay there."

"Let me know how much it will cost."

"Don't worry about it. We've got it covered. Your uncle is part of our organization that helps out with this sort of stuff."

"That's good to hear."

He helped her up and the soft touch of his hands caused a ripple of pleasure to run through her.

"Good night," he said, his voice, lower and more sensual than he'd probably intended.

"Good night," she said, and a magnetic energy drew her lips to his.

He leaned down to kiss her, his sweet lips were tingly and delicious, just as she'd imagined.

This man could kiss!

She moaned into his lips as he pleasured her with his sweetness. His lips were so soft and delicious. She wanted to taste them all night.

He nuzzled her neck with his nose and drove her wild.

"Oh, Jake," she groaned with pleasure, yet he wasn't inside her—yet.

She felt as if she'd known him forever. And although she'd intended to take a break from ever dating again, she couldn't help herself. She wanted him more than anything.

This man had saved her life!

In more ways than one. He gave her something to hope for. He made her realize that not all guys were assholes like her ex.

He was one of the good guys; one of the guys she never thought she'd ever be with.

It was as if the universe gave her another chance at finding happiness.

But she didn't want to get ahead of herself.

It was only a kiss.

But she wanted more than a kiss from sweet, sexy mountain man Jake.

The space between her legs tingled thinking of what he would feel like inside her.

"I've been wanting you from the moment I first saw you, Evie," he moaned as he continued to kiss her sensuously.

Her heart leaped with excitement in her chest on hearing this.

She could not believe Jake felt the same way she did.

Yet, she had planned to keep her distance. He was her uncle's neighbor. This was a no-no.

Her heart raced as she shivered inside with delight. The touch of his warm skin on hers sent her into pleasure overload. Heat climbed between her thighs as his gentle strokes caressed her. Her sex throbbed with want for him. She craved him. Desired him. Wanted nothing more than to be with him. All. The. Time. She didn't know if she could ever control herself around him...

Everything felt so right.

Chapter 9 - Jake

This was wrong.

What was he doing?

Evie had just had her heart broken by her ex groom. Jake wanted her, but he wanted to make sure she was okay with this.

He'd always been able to keep his feelings in check around her—until now. Were his guys right? Had he changed in this short time. Had there been a spark, a light that now shone around him? He certainly felt different. Hopeful, loved. The evening they spent together was amazing. He'd liked everything he knew about her from a year ago when her uncle told him about the type of person she was. But he was overly protective of her too. Just like Jake was.

Unlike his ex, Evie was different. For one thing, she was honest. He liked that in a girl. Not only that, but the chemistry between them was also explosive. He'd never felt that way about any woman before. Not even his ex.

Deep down, he felt she was the one.

He didn't feel that connection to any woman before. Not like Evie.

But when she reached up to him and stroked his cheek then pulled him down to meet her sweet, soft lips, he went crazy. His body was on fire for her.

He respected her. Cherished her in every way possible.

He wanted to protect her.

He also wanted to be inside her. Deep inside her.

He wanted her now.

But only if she was ready.

"Evie, maybe we shouldn't." His voice was low and hoarse with arousal.

A shadow of disappointment slid across her pretty face. He almost regretted saying that. He could tell she was just as aroused as he was. His dick was hard as a rock now, straining beneath his pants.

"You just got out of a relationship," he added.

"A relationship that never felt right. But this feels right, Jake. I want you so badly. I hadn't felt this way in forever." Her breath was rapid and deep. "What did you say about living in the moment. And acting when things felt right."

A grin curved his lips. He felt a sweet warm feeling slide inside his body.

Chapter 10 - Evie

"Oh, Evie. You have no idea what you do to me. God, I want you," he groaned with pleasure between passionate kisses.

"Jake, I want you too," she murmured with delight between tender kisses while he stroked her sensitive skin on her neck then placed his lips there. Shivers of delight slid down her back. Butterflies exploded in her belly.

His lips were so soft and she tingled at his touch as he held her gently. She ran her hands down his muscular arms. His grip was so firm, strong. Man, his muscles were ripped, so defined. She loved the firm feel underneath her fingertips as she slid her hands down his biceps.

"Are you sure you want to do this?" he said, tenderly. He lips brushed against hers then he gently led her to the couch in the living room as the fire blazed in the fireplace.

"Yes," she breathed.

He then paused.

"Is everything all right?" she asked, concerned that he was going to change his mind.

"I need to see if I have a condom."

"Of course," she said, still breathing heavily, hoping he had a condom. She wanted to go all the way with him tonight.

"I think I might have some in my truck," he said.

"Good," she said, breathless, trying to hide her excitement as the heat of passion rushed through her.

He kissed her, a cute grin on his lips as he stroked her chin, adoration for her in his eyes as he put on his jacket and went outside.

It seemed like forever for Jake to return and she wondered if he'd changed his mind, knowing that, after all, she *was* his neighbor's niece.

Would that make things awkward between them? She hoped not. She knew how her uncle felt about mixing family with his friends. He'd once told her that he introduced his youngest sister to his friend and the relationship had exploded and caused a rift between all of them. Since then her uncle was never too keen on the idea that a neighbor or friend of his would date a relative of his.

She really hoped he wouldn't be funny about this scenario. Jake was different. Her uncle knew that.

Her body was still aroused. Anticipating her night with Jake. What would he feel like inside of her? How would he sound when he came? How would she feel having a man that she adored from head to toe, a man she loved everything about. A man who made her feel so good inside, yet they hadn't even been intimate yet.

Her nipples tightened into buds as her mind ran on sexy Jake with his rock-hard abs and sculpted body. What a hot body. He must work out at the gym every day. Oh, wait. He was in the mountains. He probably just worked a lot with his hands. She just couldn't wait for them to continue what they'd just started.

She noticed a box in the corner with a tree inside. Was he planning on putting up the Christmas tree soon? She hoped so.

Talk about a hot Christmas present.

This was a holiday gift she would always remember.

She glanced out the window, hoping Jake would be back soon. Snowflakes fell outside and created a pretty picture against the night sky.

The fire continued to blaze in the cozy living room.

Everything seemed perfect.

Except...

Jake was missing.

"Jake," she called out after she opened the front door.

Just then, she heard footsteps from the side of the log cabin.

"Evie? You okay?" Jake asked as he rounded the corner.

"I'm good." *And still turned on*, she thought to herself. "Where were you?"

"Just saw a squirrel stuck under a tree branch. I set it free. Winds are crazy right now."

"I know. That was so sweet of you."

"Hey, you're going to catch a cold like that." He gestured to her as she stood in the doorway.

He took off his jacket and covered her immediately as his fingers brushed her skin. Warmth swept through her body. The scent of his sexy cologne wafted to her nose. Her body tingled from his sweet touch. But she was hungry for more of Jake. She could tell he was still aroused too as she neared him, pressing her lips to his again.

She wanted him to take her now. Right there and then on the porch. They kissed hungrily as they made their way inside and Jake kicked the door shut behind him when he got inside with her.

He was strong, handsome and charming. And so sweet underneath that tough, ruggedly handsome exterior.

"Thank you again for what you did," she whispered, feeling waves of appreciation and desire for him washing over her.

"What did I do?" he moaned, playfully.

"For rescuing me earlier," she said. "For saving my uncle's cabin. For being there for me when I was feeling so down. I've always wanted to follow my heart and do something fun and exciting. You were there for me...and I want you..."

"Hey, I'm glad you're all right," he said in a deep sexy voice that slid right through her body.

"Is this what they mean by the magic of the Christmas season?" she asked, playfully as they continued to make out. She loved that she could feel his hard erection underneath his pants as his strong, warm body pressed into hers. Oh, she wanted him now.

He grinned and a sexy dimple appeared on his cheek. Man, he was gorgeous. He was so sexy; it was distracting her—in a good way. And she loved his rich silky voice. She could listen to him all night long.

What would her uncle think? Right now, she didn't want to worry about that. She cared about how she felt in the moment. That magnetic chemistry between them was undeniable. It felt so good.

"So, did you find a condom?" she asked, hopefully.

A grin curved his sexy lips. "I sure did."

Relief washed over her. She was so glad and couldn't wait to feel Jake's cock inside her.

"What's on your sweet mind?" he asked in a deep sexy voice.

"I want you, Jake," she whispered, passionately.

She leaned into him and felt his hard erection through his pants.

"What do you want me to do right now?" A sexy grin curved his sensuous lips, his voice was low and deep.

"Everything," she whispered seductively, breathless.

"I'll take it slow, beautiful," he said, kissing her shoulders then trailing his lips down further as her body quivered with excitement and anticipation of more.

Man, this guy could kiss. Where did he learn to do that with his lips?

"I want you," she breathed.

He pressed his lips to her neck and ran his soft firm fingers down her back. She loved the way she felt with him. She'd never felt this magic with her ex before. Jake was different. He was everything her ex was not. But most of all, she loved the look of love in his eyes when he gazed into hers. She loved the way he cherished her with his eyes, his words, his touch. He was so gentle, yet strong. So sweet, yet caring.

"I know this might sound crazy," she said, softly. "But I think you're the man I've been waiting for my whole life."

He grinned appreciatively. "You know, I was thinking the same thing about you being the woman I've always dreamed of. I've never felt this way about any woman before."

She kissed him hungrily and he kissed her back with as much passion. His lips were so soft.

"I don't have a lot of experience," she said, breathing hard, wanting him more than anything.

"Is this your first time?" He looked alarmed.

"I was supposed to be the reality TV virgin bride," she admitted, biting down on her lower lip.

"Oh, Evie. I had no idea. Are you sure you want to do this now? Here?"

"Yes," she grinned. "I want you now. Right here. The mood is so right. This is so unplanned," she said, between hot kisses on his lips. "I've always planned everything out in the perfect moment and the perfect location. Well, I want to try something new and spontaneous."

He kissed her with heated passion.

"I had doubts with my ex, but not with you, Jake," she said, breathless. "This feels right to me. Oh, you feel so good."

His sweet scent drove her nuts. She wanted him now.

The space between her legs pulsed with excitement. He couldn't possibly stop now.

If Jake wasn't inside her soon, she'd go crazy out of her mind.

Everything felt so right with Jake.

"I promise to be gentle, Evie. You're so precious and beautiful. You're the most amazing woman I've ever met," he said, softly brushing his fingers against her skin. "I want to make love to you in ways you would never imagine."

She groaned with delight.

Jake tenderly stripped her out of her clothes as he kissed her tenderly, each area of her exposed skin. Then slid off her lace panties. A low groan of approval and desire slipped through his sexy lips. She was glad she wore her silk and lace panties tonight. Thank goodness for that.

He then caressed her skin with his lips as his hands slid over her body. He then circled her nipple on her right breast while stroking her other nipple with his wet tongue. She moaned with delight as the sensation slid throughout her body.

Evie dug her fingers into Jake's strong muscular back, enjoying his physique, his sexy body.

Moments later, he guided her down on the soft sofa and continued to pleasure her with his lips. The fire in the fireplace blazed. It was warm and comfortable. Romantic.

"How do you like that?" he said, his voice hoarse with arousal after he sucked on one and then her other nipple while her pussy throbbed with arousal.

She groaned with ecstasy.

He gazed lovingly into her eyes as he slowly moved his fingers down between her legs, stroking her gently.

"Oh, you're so wet," he groaned with hoarseness, his lips curved into a grin.

He then slid one finger inside her, moving slowly at first then he added another finger and slid deep inside her back and forth as she writhed beneath him.

He then lowered his lips to her pussy folds and sucked on her sensitive skin, softly and rhythmically while she responded with arousal. Butterflies slid throughout her belly. The sensation was amazing. She wanted more. She begged for more. But she wanted his hardness inside her now.

She grabbed the cushions to her sides on the sofa as he went down on her again and again.

He French kissed her sex. Pleasure filled her pussy as his wet tongue now caressed her inner thighs with expertise.

Jake's gorgeous face was sweetly between her legs, licking her off. She was going to come. God, he was amazing! How did he learn to pleasure a woman like that. The buildup was pulsing.

She arched her back in response as he thrust his tongue inside her, swirling and teasing her wet throbbing pussy, kissing her sex with hunger and passion.

"I'm going to come," she cried out. "Oh, Jake."

She'd never had anyone down there before. She loved the way his lips felt on her.

She was thrilled to be sharing this moment with him.

"You like that, baby?"

"Yes, oh, yes," she groaned with arousal.

He sucked faster and harder, licking her until she came with an intense wave of orgasm. Her legs trembled.

"Oh, Jake," she breathed hard. "Amazing. You're amazing."

"You are, beautiful," he said, his voice hoarse with arousal.

He got up, his pants tented with his erection.

She reached over and unbuckled his belt, seductively.

He helped her and soon his pants and silk boxers were off.

Her eyes widened with delight.

His cock was huge!

His body was even more stunning naked. She admired his physique; the muscular V shape of his thighs was impressive.

She couldn't wait to take him in. She could see the desire in his lovely blue eyes and that turned her on even more.

She stroked Jake's cock up and down with her hand as he groaned with pleasure. His precum moistening her hand. She'd learned about how to do this though she'd never actually done it before.

Slowly, she moved her lips towards the tip of his erection then she took him into her mouth.

"God," he groaned out loud.

His skin tasted clean with a hint of soap. She took him in deeper into her moist mouth as he moved gently inside her. He was so gentle as he controlled his movements, her lips wrapped firmly around his hardness.

He stopped her before he came. He then reached into his pants on the floor and pulled out a condom from the pocket. Before long, he rolled his condom on. She was thrilled that he'd had a condom on him because she really wanted to go all the way tonight.

Still hard, Jake positioned himself over her, kissing her softly and tenderly. First on her lips then down her neck. She could taste her own sex on his soft lips.

"God, I want you now," he moaned. "You ready?" he asked.

"Yes, please. Now. I want you now, Jake," she said, breathing hard. She could hear their hearts thumping fast.

He then repositioned himself again and lined up his huge dick to her small opening.

"You are so beautiful, Evie," he breathed, his voice hoarse with arousal.

She moaned in response to him as he continued to plant sweet kisses on her sensitive skin.

A wave of pleasure swept through her entire body as she trembled when he first moved slowly inside her.

Man, it felt so good. He filled her completely as he gently kissed her and told her how much he truly cared about her and how beautiful she was.

She French kissed him back, hungrily.

He thrust inside her going deeper and deeper, moving his hips in a sweet rhythmic motion as he made love to her. Moments later, he thrust faster inside her as she begged for more, feeling intense pleasure roll through her body.

He rocked back and forth and soon she came with an intense orgasm. Jake came soon after, muscles spasming with pleasure.

Breathing hard and fast they cuddled with each other.

"You okay, beautiful," he breathed.

"Yes. More than okay. That was so amazing, Jake," she moaned as she brushed her lips over his.

This moment was so magical. She didn't want this moment to end. Jake hugged her snuggly. His warm body over hers, his sweet cologne scent wafting to her nose. She loved this moment. She loved Jake. But...she couldn't help but wonder now.

What was going to happen next?

Chapter 11 - Jake

The next morning, Jake watched as Evie slept. He was mesmerized by her beauty, but he tried to stay focused.

Her uncle was going to kill him.

He wanted Evie now more than ever.

But did she feel the same way about him? Or was this just about one night. It was up to Evie what happened next. But he thought he'd go crazy inside if he couldn't see her again after tonight. He'd go insane. And he never felt this way about his ex. In fact, the love-making was magical with Evie. His body still buzzed with intense pleasure, excitement. Filled with the afterglow of their love.

He got up, leaving his beautiful queen sleeping in his bed. He was going to make breakfast for his curvaceous sleeping beauty.

Evie

Later that morning, Evie woke up, a smile on her face, feeling good for the first time in a long while. Her pussy felt pleasurably sore. Last night, Jake had temporarily placed a cool wash cloth on her inner folds for a few minutes after they'd made love. He knew what to do to cool her off. He was so expert in everything. He always knew what to do. She reached over to the other side of the bed and found a warm empty side.

The scrumptious scent of bacon and eggs frying in the kitchen wafted to her nostrils. Did he seriously make breakfast for her too?

Jake was phenomenal.

The thought of leaving him and going to her uncle's cabin dampened her mood.

She wanted to spend more time with Jake.

She wanted him. All of him.

She ran over her *Soul Mate Wish List* in her mind.

He ticked all the boxes.

He was the one.

Later, they both sat down to breakfast overlooking the lovely greenery outside through the log cabin's tall windows. There was a light dusting of white snowflakes from last night's snow fall. It was relaxing, serene. But that had a lot to do with her impressive host.

"This is the most delicious breakfast, or rather, brunch, I've ever tasted," she said. Their brunch included fresh strawberries with fluffy pancakes and lightly tossed scrambled eggs with bacon. And there was a rose on the table. How sweet. What a romantic gesture.

"I'm glad you like it." His morning voice was deep and sexy and turned her on.

"I love it. I love being with you." Why did she just blurt that out? Was Jake just a one-night stand? Where did they stand?

"I love being with you too last night, Evie. I'm so honored to be your first. You're so beautiful. And you're a queen. I would love to be more than that," he said, his sexy ocean-blue eyes penetrating hers. Her heart turned over in her chest with excitement.

He was her dream boyfriend. He was a good man. He was respectful and gentle with her. He was also an amazing cook. Great in the kitchen. Great in the bedroom. What more could she ask for?

She was full in every way possible. Her heart, her soul, her tummy. Yet she wanted more of sweet and sexy Jake.

Later, they talked by the fireplace as they watched the snow fall again outside. What a magical moment in the mountains with an impressively hot mountain man.

Why couldn't this last?

Heat climbed to Evie's cheeks. The space between her thighs jumped just thinking about the deep penetration she'd had with Jake. And the passion.

The warmth.

The connection.

The chemistry.

When she ran her mind over her *Soul Mate Wish List* she realized she had it all with Jake—and wanted to be his dream soul mate too. The wish list was a fun experiment she'd created on her blog for her followers. They would each talk about their perfect soul mate and how they too could be the perfect soul mate for that special person. He had it all, didn't he? So what was she worried about?

Jake was:

1. Sweet and sexy
2. Loved her for who she was – he admired her curves. He didn't tell her she had to lose weight like her ex had told her.
3. A passionate kisser
4. He was amazing in bed
5. He made her heart race every time she was near him, he took her breath away
6. He was strong and so kind
7. He was faithful and honest
8. He was great in the kitchen, not just in the bedroom
9. He was a great listener

She'd always wanted to do something spontaneous and follow her heart. So why not now?

Moments later, he neared her again and pressed his lips to hers. Man, his lips felt so good.

"Jake, I had an amazing time last night."

"So did I. I think I'm in love with you, Evie," he said in a deep, sensuous voice. "I know we haven't known each other long..."

"I knew my ex way longer than that and looked at how that turned out," she said. "I want us to make a go of it. I've had more fun with you in the last twenty-four hours than I've had with my ex in a year."

"Same here. And I'm glad you're not going to give up on your business. Don't let that guy ruin what you've built. If I've learned anything from the army is that as long as you have breath in your body—it's not over."

The words struck her like a harmonious chord. "You know something, Jake, you're right. What have I got to lose."

"And I'm right here for you, if you ever need me," he added, holding her from behind. His strong arms wrapped around her.

A smile of appreciation curved her lips. "Thank you, Jake." Her ex had never been so kind to her.

"You know something I think I will turn comments back on my social media accounts. I'm going to work on a new post titled: *Second Chances. It's never too late*." She grinned. The irony of where Jake's log cabin was located wasn't lost on her either.

"What better place than Second Chance Lane," he said.

"I wonder if that's why the Lanes named it Second Chance."

"You know something, you're onto something. I think legend had it that Mr. Lane came back from the second World War and was happy to be able to marry his fiancée. They moved out here and he built a few cabins around here. The mayor named the street after him for his bravery and service in the war. And he was thankful and asked if the street could be called Second Chance Lane."

"What a beautiful love story," she said, her heart melting with warmth and joy.

"Sure is. As beautiful as you."

She chuckled, warmly. "I think this place is sensational." She glanced lovingly into his sexy blue eyes. "I think you're magical."

"*You're* the magical beauty," he said. "I never thought I'd give love a second chance but...I love the way you make me feel. I feel so alive around you...I've fallen in love with you."

"I've fallen in love with you too."

"Stay here with me," he said, his expression sincere. "I want to spend more time with you. See where this leads. I've never felt this way about anyone before."

The words caused her heart to leap in her chest. "I will. Right here is where I want to be." She reached her arms around the back of his neck. "With you."

***

Thank you for reading *Rescued by the Mountain Man* (Mountain Men of Charming Falls): Jake and Evie's love story.

Want to read about more magical romances in this quaint small mountain town? Will ex-military mountain man and volunteer builder Erik find his happily ever after in Charming Falls? Read Book 2 in Mountain Men of Charming Falls – Claimed by the Mountain Man. Available now!

Books by Ann Ric

Mountain Men of Charming Falls
    Rescued by the Mountain Man (Evie & Jake)
    Claimed by the Mountain Man (Candi & Erik)
    Stranded with the Mountain Man (Lilly & Alex)
    Christmas with the Mountain Man (Harmony & Chase)

Magic Protector Reverse Harem Trilogy
    Magic Protector – A Steamy Paranormal Reverse Harem Romance (Book 1)
    Magic Bound – A Steamy Paranormal Reverse Harem Romance (Book 2)
    Magic Promise – A Steamy Paranormal Reverse Harem Romance (Book 3)

ABOUT THE AUTHOR

Ann Ric enjoys writing steamy paranormal romance novels and sizzling hot contemporary romance short stories with a happily ever after. She loves to read romance novels featuring strong characters and breathtaking worlds. You can reach her by email at heartandsoulbooks7@gmail.com